PIRASAURS!

For GG, because no one I know lived closer to
the age of the dinosaurs than you. — J.F.

To Michael Fleming — A good bucko who knows
whar thee treasure is buried. — M.S.

Text copyright © 2016 by Josh Funk
Illustrations copyright © 2016 by Michael Slack

ISBN 978-1-338-13204-5

10 9 8 7 6 5 4 3 2 1   16 17 18 19 20

Printed in the U.S.A. 08
First printing 2016
The text type was set in Dry Cowboy.

Book design by Jess Tice-Gilbert and Patti Ann Harris

PIRASAURS!

By Josh Funk

Illustrations by Michael Slack

Scholastic Inc.

We're Pirasaurs!
We're Pirasaurs!
We rule the open seas!

We'll cannon-blast you to the past!
We do just what we please!

With spiky tails, we raise the sails
To search for gold and more!

We must beware, for everywhere
Are enemies galore!

With lots to learn,
I've got to earn
The crew's respect and trust.

I'll rise in rank or
Walk the plank...
I hope I can adjust!

When Captain Rex says

Swab the decks!

She points her fabled sword.

I scrub and brush in such a rush
She throws me overboard!

The ship is steered by Bronto Beard.
He serves as lookout, too!
His single eye spots far and nigh,
When I see only blue!

With handy hook, Triceracook
Prepares Jurassic feasts!

BURP

I love to slurp and belch and burp
With buccaneering beasts!

Velocimate can navigate
From reef to coastal bay.

I use my smarts to map the charts.

But still we're led astray!

Our ancient ship will rise and dip
Across the sea frontier.
We boldly row until "Land ho!"
The treasure must be near.

When Captain Rex says
"Find the X!"

I haven't got a clue.

Beside them all, I feel quite small.
I'm still so very new.

The crew begins to search within
The frayed and tattered map,
A shadow looms, the water fumes
Revealing—

It's a trap!

From sky and sea—it couldn't be . . .
Another dino crew?
Yo ho! Behold! They want the gold!
These scallywags are through!

As Captain Rex's muscles flex
She readies sword and claws!
Velocimate can barely wait
And bares his golden jaws!

Kablamo! Crash!

A mighty clash
Erupts upon the sand.

But then I spot a bandit's got
A piece of map in hand.

I blurt at last.
"We've got to stop these duels!

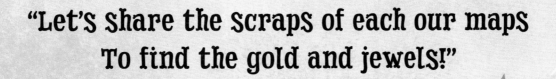

"Let's share the scraps of each our maps
To find the gold and jewels!"

Surprisingly, they stare at me,
But nobody objects.
The maps connect and they reflect
The spot that's marked with X.

It's been my dream to join the team.
This crew and I are linked.
With gems, doubloons, and silver spoons
We'll never go extinct!

Through battles, brawls, and fireballs,
Plus prehistoric roars,
The salty deep is ours to keep—